Don't let the Joker take over the whole book. Build the Batman minifigure, and he'll soon show him who's boss!

WHAT THIS BOOK NEEDS IS A REAL CRIMINAL. HERE'S MY CARD!

WELCOME TO GOTHAM CITY ...

IF YOU THINK YOU'RE ABOUT TO VISIT A QUIET AND PEACEFUL PLACE, YOU'RE GRAVELY MISTAKEN!

WHEREVER YOU GO IN GOTHAM CITY, YOU'RE BOUND TO BUMP INTO SOME CRIMINALS OR WITNESS A ROBBERY.

I'M GLAD YOU'RE ALL HERE. TIME TO SAY HI, GREEN LANTERN!

THIS ISN'T FUNNY AT ALL!

GREAT TRAP, BATMAN! LET'S DO IT AGAIN SOME TIME!

I DON'T THINK SO!

REALLY. WHY?

YOU DON'T LOOK AS GOOD AS I DO IN MY OUTFIT.

THE END

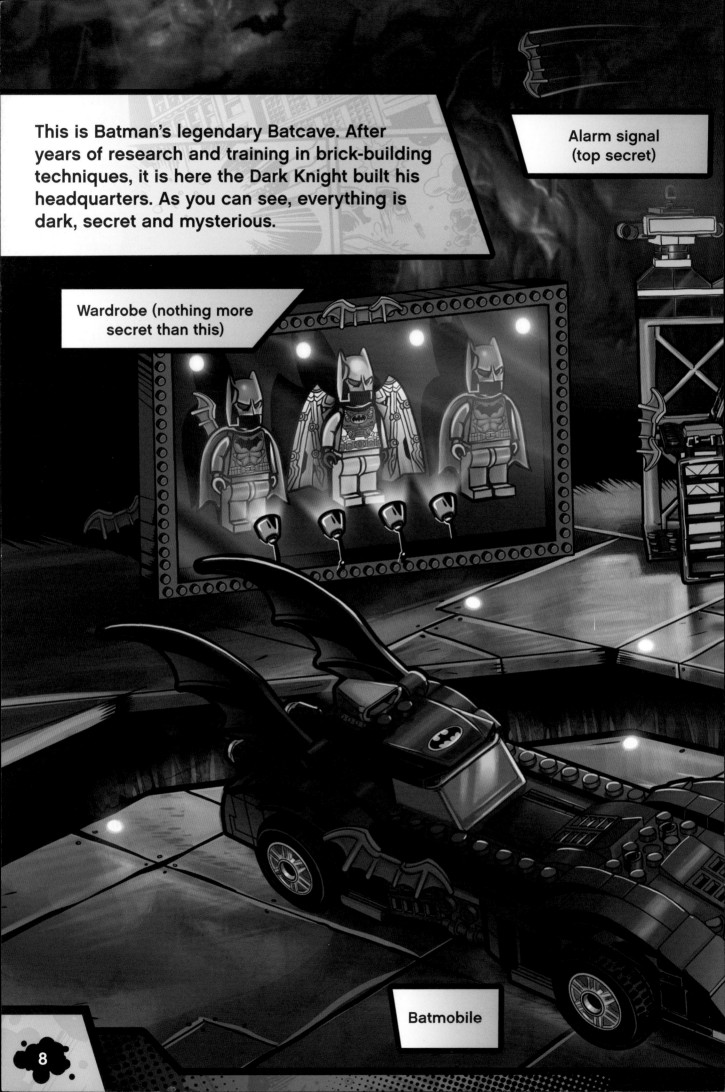

This is Batman's legendary Batcave. After years of research and training in brick-building techniques, it is here the Dark Knight built his headquarters. As you can see, everything is dark, secret and mysterious.

Alarm signal (top secret)

Wardrobe (nothing more secret than this)

Batmobile

8

GOTHAM CITY CHASE!

BREAKING NEWS ... ROBBERY OF THE CENTURY IN GOTHAM CITY! TWO-FACE AND HIS GANG HAVE STOLEN A WHOLE SAFE FROM A BANK ...

THEY BLEW UP THE BANK'S WALL AND ARE NOW RACING THROUGH THE STREETS OF GOTHAM CITY!

THERE ARE BRICKS EVERYWHERE. SOMEONE HAD BETTER CALL BATMAN!

DAILY PLANET NEWS

What route should Batman take to reach the city centre as fast as possible?

START

FINISH

READY FOR SOME ACTION?

I AM. YOU GO AND FINISH YOUR HOMEWORK.

If Batman wants to catch Two-Face, he'll need to find his way between the buildings of Gotham City. Can you help him?

FINISH

Two-Face has hidden the safe in the Gotham City sewer. Show Batman how to find it, then catch the whole gang. Look out for the pipes leading to the hungry alligators!

START

FINISH

15

There's one last thing that has to be done to catch Two-Face and his gang. Help Batman through the maze to track them down.

I BET YOU'RE GETTING SCARED NOW!

START

I THINK I'LL TOSS A COIN TO SEE IF I MAKE IT!

FINISH

ATTACK ON GOTHAM CITY!

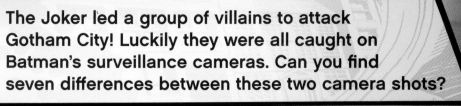

The Joker led a group of villains to attack Gotham City! Luckily they were all caught on Batman's surveillance cameras. Can you find seven differences between these two camera shots?

The Joker and his henchmen are planning to rob a bank. Untangle the speech bubble lines to help Batman foil the bank robbery.

HAS ANYONE SEEN SUPERMAN? I WANT TO GET HIS AUTOGRAPH.

LEAVE MY BRICKS ALONE. I NEED TO FIX MY CAR!

DRAMATIC INTRO

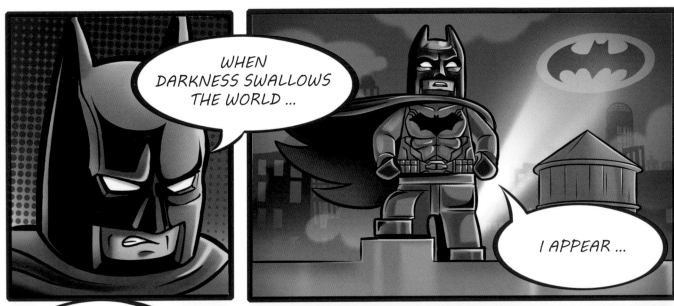

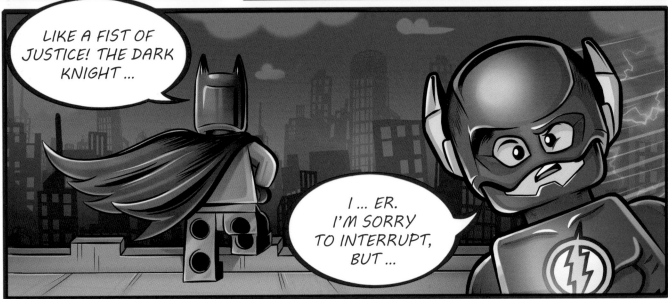

The Justice League has arrived in Gotham City! There are four small pictures on the page, but the League only needs one of them to be ready to go. Which one is it?

A

B

C

D

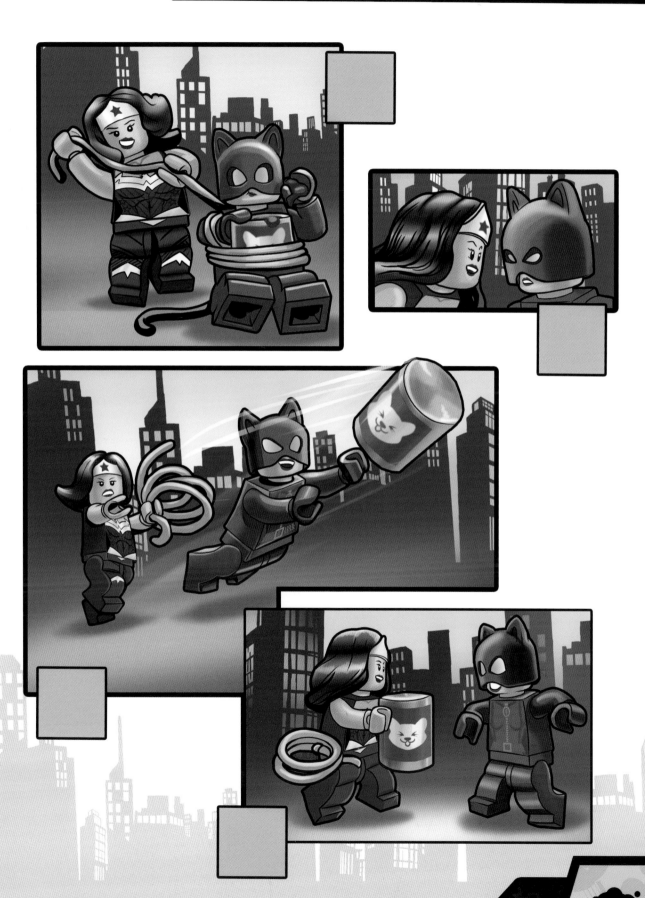

The Joker and his gang are hiding in a toyshop. Can you spot all four villains? Then count how many clown toys there are.

WHY IS BATMAN THE GREATEST SUPER HERO?

BECAUSE HE'S BATMAN!

It may sound obvious, but it's true! Here's why Batman is the greatest super hero – simply by being himself.

REASON #1:

He has a knack for making a REALLY great entrance.

REASON #2:

Everyone wants Batman's costume ... and he knows it!

REASON #3:

He's the World's Greatest Detective.

REASON #4:

His Bat-Signal is just awesome!

REASON #5:

His greatest enemy is the Joker, the most dangerous villain of all!

REASON #6:

He's got a really deep voice!

REASON #7:

Somehow he's always where he's needed!

REASON #8:

The most important reason: everyone wants to be Batman!

The Joker wants to keep his mugshot as a souvenir. Can you find one that's identical to the large image of him?

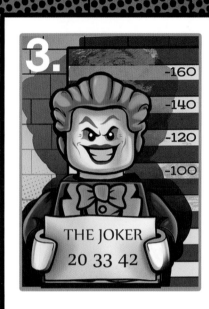

ANSWERS

p. 8–9

p. 11

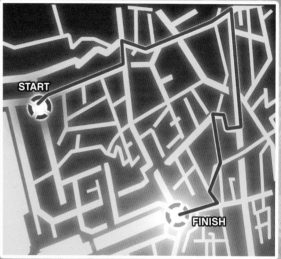

p. 12–13

p. 14–15

p. 16

One route you can take is as follows:

p. 18–19

p. 20–21

p. 24

p. 26–27

= 18

p. 25

2.

-160
-140
-120
-100

THE JOKER
20 33 42